Published by Ladybird Books Ltd
Penguin Books Ltd, 80 Strand, London WC2R 0RL, England
Penguin (Group) Australia, 250 Camberwell Road, Camberwell, Victoria 3124, Australia
Penguin Group (NZ), cnr Airborne and Rosedale Roads, Albany, Auckland 1310,
New Zealand
A Penguin Company

1 3 5 7 9 10 8 6 4 2
This presentation copyright © Ladybird Books Ltd, 2006
New reproductions of Beatrix Potter's book illustrations copyright © Frederick Warne & Co.,
2002
Original text and illustrations copyright © Frederick Warne & Co., 1902

Additional illustrations by Colin Twinn and Alex Vining

Frederick Warne & Co. is the owner of all rights, copyrights and trademarks in the Beatrix
Potter character names and illustrations.

ISBN-13: 978-1-8464-6353-2
ISBN-10: 1-8464-6353-X

Printed in Italy

THE TALE OF
PETER RABBIT

A SIMPLIFIED RETELLING OF THE ORIGINAL TALE BY
BEATRIX POTTER

This is Peter Rabbit.

He lives here with his mother, Mrs Rabbit, and his sisters, Flopsy, Mopsy and Cotton-tail.

One morning Mrs Rabbit said, "I am going out, children. Now run along, but don't go into Mr McGregor's garden."

Then Mrs Rabbit took her
basket and her umbrella and
walked through the wood.

Flopsy, Mopsy and
Cotton-tail were good
little rabbits. They went
to pick blackberries.

But Peter was a naughty
little rabbit. He ran to
Mr McGregor's garden
and squeezed under
the gate!

Peter sat in the garden and ate lots of radishes.

Then, feeling rather sick, he
went to look for some parsley
to make him feel better.

But round the corner he
met . . .

... Mr McGregor!

Mr McGregor ran after
Peter Rabbit, waving a
rake and shouting,
"Stop thief!"

Peter ran into a net and got
caught by the buttons on his
blue jacket.

Then Mr McGregor tried
to trap Peter with a sieve!

Peter wriggled out but he
lost his jacket and shoes.

Peter jumped into a
watering-can.

Mr McGregor was looking
for him underneath
the flowerpots.

Then Peter jumped out of
a window and knocked
over some flowerpots.
He got away!

Mr McGregor was tired
of running after Peter.

He went back to his work.

Peter heard the *scritch*, *scratch* of Mr McGregor's hoe. He climbed on to a wheelbarrow and looked across the garden.

He could see the gate!

Peter ran as fast as he could go. Mr McGregor saw him but Peter didn't care. He slipped under the gate and was safe at last.

When Peter got home, he was so tired that he flopped down on to the floor.

Mrs Rabbit was cooking. "Where have you been, Peter Rabbit?" she said.

Peter Rabbit was not very well. Mrs Rabbit put him to bed and made him some tea.

But Flopsy, Mopsy and
Cotton-tail had bread
and milk and blackberries
for supper.